© 2024 Quarto Publishing Group USA Inc.
Text and illustrations © 2024 Fred Blunt

Fred Blunt has asserted his right to be identified as the author and illustrator of this work.

Senior Designer: Sarah Chapman-Suire
Commissioning Editors: Emily Pither and Catharine Robertson
Creative Director: Malena Stojić
Associate Publisher: Rhiannon Findlay
Production Manager: Nikki Ingram

First published in 2024 by Happy Yak, an imprint of The Quarto Group.
100 Cummings Center, Suite 265D
Beverly, MA 01915, USA
T (978) 282-9590 F (978) 283-2742
www.quarto.com

No part of this publication may be reproduced, stored in a retrieval system, or transmitted in any form, or by any means, electrical, mechanical, photocopying, recording, or otherwise, without the prior written permission of the publisher or a license permitting restricted copying.

All rights reserved.

A CIP record for this book is available from the Library of Congress.

ISBN: 978-0-7112-9063-1
Manufactured in Guangdong, China CC042024
9 8 7 6 5 4 3 2 1

In memory of Olive, Rusty, and Ben—F.B.

The End.

Fine, I'll prove it—watch this.

Sit.

Roll over.

See what I mean?

Surprisingly, they have an amazing sense of smell...

...but just look how they use it!

Dogs will chase anything that moves...

...even their own tail!

Did I mention they were stupid?

small...

wrinkly...

pinkly...

mop...

Hairy...

scary...

spotty...

Scottie...

stuffy... scruffy... ...ever so fluffy!

You won't mistake a cat for a hot dog, that's for sure.

See: a cat.

Another cat.

You know what you're getting with cats.

No big surprises.

BUM

Errrr, BIG CAT!!
Nice kitty?

Actually, there is one good thing about dogs...

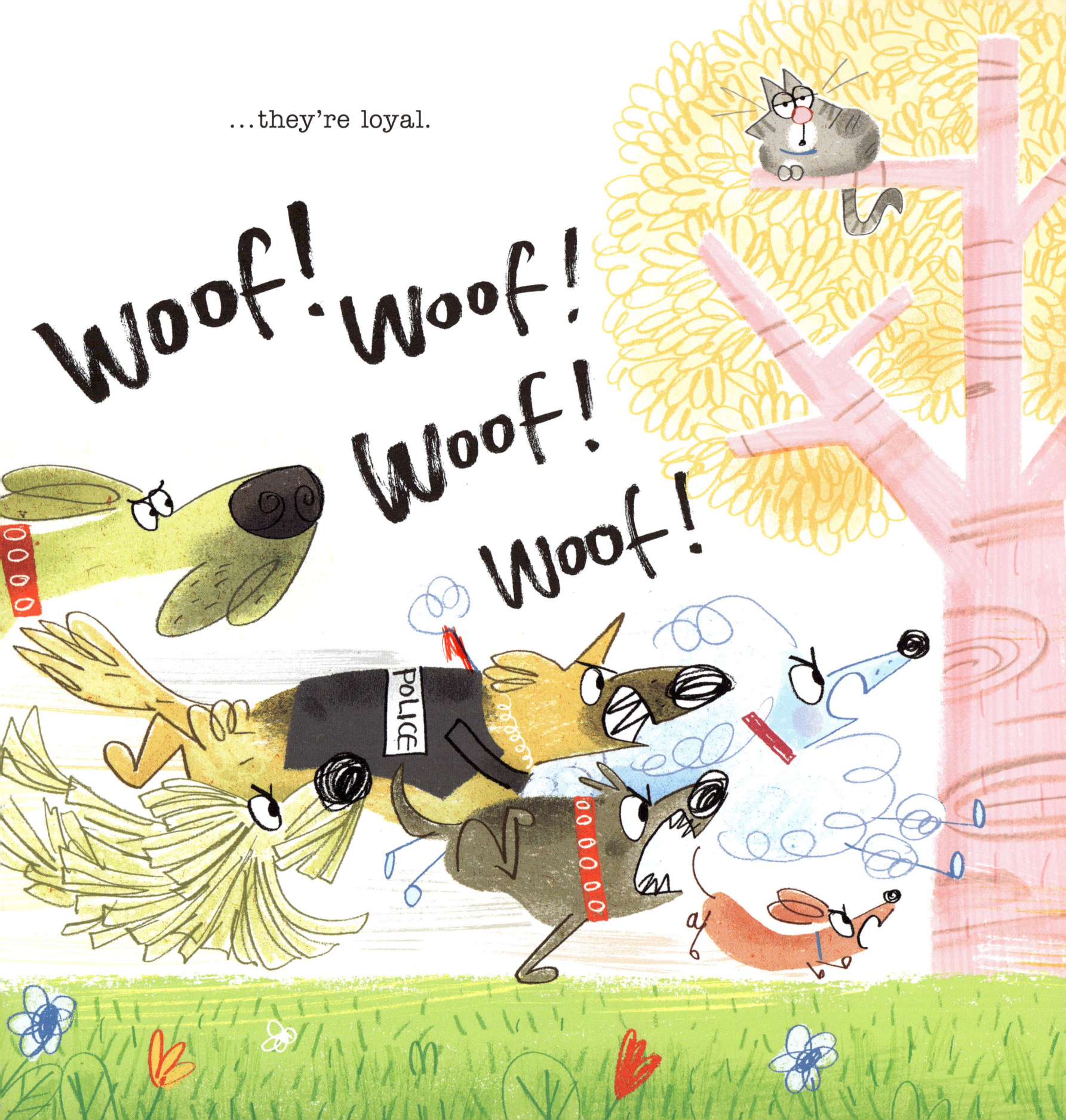

In fact...

...a dog is the best friend you can have.*

The End.

(*Just don't tell anyone I said that.)

ZOO